Dinosaurs
of All Sizes

Dr. Alvin Granowsky

RSVP
RAINTREE
STECK-VAUGHN
PUBLISHERS
The Steck-Vaughn Company

Austin, Texas

**Illustrations by
Paul Lopez**

The name dinosaur means "terrible lizard."
But that isn't a very good name for the strange
reptiles that lived a long, long time ago.

2

Some dinosaurs were huge and scary.
Just think of a Triceratops or a Tyrannosaurus.
The name "terrible" fits them.
They **were** terrible!

But some dinosaurs were very little.
They ate only plants and were not fierce at all.

The second part of the name dinosaur
means "lizard."
But today scientists know that dinosaurs
were not really lizards.

In some ways, dinosaurs were like all reptiles.
They had dry, scaly skin and
they had a backbone.
They even lived during a time
called the Age of Reptiles.

There were many kinds of reptiles
during the Age of Reptiles.
Some reptiles had wings to fly.
Some reptiles swam in the sea.
Some reptiles lived on land.

Many people think all of these reptiles
were dinosaurs.
But that is not true!

Dinosaurs were different from all other reptiles.
The way they stood and the way they walked
made them different.

Some reptiles creep.
Look at the way a crocodile or a turtle moves.
Their body drags along the ground as they crawl.
Their legs stand out from their sides.

10

A dinosaur stood with its legs
straight under its body.
A dinosaur did not drag its body on the ground.

Dinosaurs lived on land.
They did not have wings to fly.
They did not have fins to swim.

12

Some dinosaurs walked on two legs
and some dinosaurs walked on four legs.
But to be called a dinosaur, a reptile had to walk
with its legs straight under its body.

To be called a dinosaur, a reptile had to walk with its body up off the ground.

To be called a dinosaur, a reptile
had to live on land.

Look at the reptiles on this page.
They lived millions of years ago
during the Age of Reptiles.
Which of these reptiles were dinosaurs?

During the Age of Reptiles, dinosaurs
of all sizes lived on Earth.

Some dinosaurs were as small as a dog.

Other dinosaurs were the biggest animals
that ever walked on land.

19

The Ceratosaurus grew as long as 20 feet.
It was a big, meat-eating dinosaur.

The Allosaurus was even bigger.
It was almost 40 feet long.
That is longer than a firetruck!

The biggest meat-eater of all was the
Tyrannosaurus Rex.
It grew as long as 46 feet and weighed
more than 7 tons.
The Tyrannosaurus is sometimes called
the king of dinosaurs.

Today we call the lion the king of beasts.
But 35 lions would not weigh as much
as one Tyrannosaurus.

The Tyrannosaurus used its strong jaws
and big body to attack other dinosaurs.
Its long, sharp teeth made the Tyrannosaurus
one of the scariest animals that ever lived.

But the largest dinosaurs were plant-eaters.
The Diplodocus was almost 90 feet long,
including its long, thin tail.

The Apatosaurus was not as long
as the Diplodocus, but it was much heavier.
It is often called a Brontosaurus,
which means "thunder lizard."

The Apatosaurus was so big that the ground
rumbled like thunder when it walked.
From the tip of its nose to the end of its tail,
the Apatosaurus was about 70 feet long.

How long is 70 feet?
Think of five big elephants standing in a line.
Then add a baby elephant to the line.
An Apatosaurus was that long.

An Apatosaurus weighed 30 tons.
That is as heavy as five big elephants!

But there were even bigger dinosaurs.
The giant Brachiosaurus was heavier
than ten elephants!
It was 74 feet long.

The Brachiosaurus was taller than
a three-story building.
But scientists have found bones
from an even bigger dinosaur.

It is called the Ultrasaurus.
The Ultrasaurus was close to 100 feet long and
may have weighed more than 20 elephants!
Someday scientists may find the fossils
of even bigger dinosaurs.

Look for these animals in
━━ Dinosaurs of All Sizes ━━

Allosaurus
(al uh SAWR uhs)
9,18,21,21

Dromaeosaurus
(droh mee oh SAWR uhs)
2, 16

Maiasaura
(my uh SAWR uh)
2, 13

Ankylosaurus
(an KY luh sawr uhs)
5,15,16

Diplodocus
(duh PLAHD uh kuhs)
25, 25, 26

Stegosaurus
(stehg uh SAWR uhs)
1, 6, 9, 19

Apatosaurus
(a pat uh SAWR uhs)
8, 19, 26-29, 26-29

Hylaeosaurus
(hy lee uh SAWR uhs)
11

Triceratops
(try SEHR uh tahps)
3, 3, **7, 14, 24**

Brachiosaurus
(brak ee uh SAWR uhs)
17, 30-31, 30-31

Iguanodon
(ih GWAHN uh dahn)
11

Tyrannosaurus
(tih ran uh SAWR uhs)
3, 3, **22,** 22, **23,** 23, **24,** 24, 25

Ceratosaurus
(sehr uh tuh SAWR uhs)
20, 20

Lesothosaurus
(luh soh toh SAWR uhs)
4

Ultrasaurus
(uhl truh SAWR uhs)
32, 32

Boldface type indicates that the animal appears in an illustration.

Acknowledgments
Design and Production: Design Five, N.Y.
Illustrations: Paul Lopez
Line Art: John Harrison

Staff Credits
Executive Editor: Elizabeth Strauss
Project Editor: Becky Ward
Project Manager: Sharon Golden

Trade Edition published 1992 © Steck-Vaughn Company
Library of Congress Cataloging-in-Publication Data
Granowsky, Alvin, 1936-
    Dinosaurs of all sizes / written by Alvin Granowsky: illustrated by Paul Lopez.
        p. cm. — (World of dinosaurs)
    Includes index.
    Summary: Describes the various sizes of dinosaurs, including Tyrannosaurus Rex,
Diplodocus, and Brontosaurus, as well as some dinosaurs that were as small as dogs.
    ISBN 0-8114-6229-3
    1. Dinosaurs — Juvenile literature. [1. Dinosaurs.] I. Lopez, Paul, ill. II. Title. III. Series.
QE862.D5G7324   1992   91-22343
567.9'7 — dc20   CIP AC